To . . . .
The star of the story!
From

T5-ANR-483

It's Christmas Eve and
. . . . .and his family
are at the North Pole to
see the reindeer.

. . . . is a little bit grumpy,
he wanted to see Santa Claus
as well, but Santa is FAR too
busy preparing to deliver
all the presents.

Grumpy . . . . kicks a clump of snow over one of the reindeer.

"Oh . . . ., that's naughty, Santa Claus only visits good children, not naughty ones. You won't be on his good list!" . . . . is reprimanded.

. . . . .kicks another clump of snow at the reindeer.

Whoops!

This time he slips and starts sliding down a snowy slope! He zips in and out of trees, faster and faster, round and down he zooms.

Suddenly, the slope transforms into a big red slide......... whizzes round and round. It's so much fun, but where is he going to end up?

He zips right off the
end of the slide and
lands perfectly into
a bright red and
green Elf suit.

. . . .'s eyes
shine with
delight. He's in
Santa's Grotto!

★ Welcome
to the Grotto

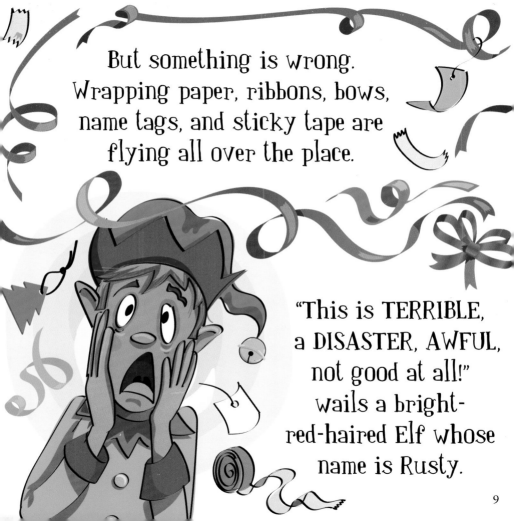

But something is wrong. Wrapping paper, ribbons, bows, name tags, and sticky tape are flying all over the place.

"This is TERRIBLE, a DISASTER, AWFUL, not good at all!" wails a bright-red-haired Elf whose name is Rusty.

9

"Whatever is the matter?" asks . . . .

Rusty peers at the oddly tall Elf and exclaims "The GOOD list is MISSING, VANISHED, DISAPPEARED! Without it, the good girls and boys won't get their presents!"

"Oh dear, that just won't do." says
. . . . "Please let me help you,
I'm great at finding things."

So Rusty takes . . . .
to the post room, where all the
letters to Santa arrive and where the incredibly
special good list is decided and written
down very carefully in glittery ink.

11

. . . . and Rusty look in the recycling containers...

...they search in the ribbon cupboard and explore under the gift boxes.

. . . . even checks inside the oven, but the good list isn't there.

. . . . asks the other Elves if they have seen the list, but they all shake their heads.

13

When . . . .
and Rusty head outside to
check with the snowman,
. . . . hears loud
chewing and
chomping coming
from the stable
where the
reindeer live.

14

They see Comet and Cupid chewing on both ends of a long piece of paper. It looks suspiciously like a list!

"Oh NO, this is TERRIBLE!" cries Rusty.

. . . . rushes to grab it and as he reads, he is extremely relieved to see what is written on it.

2 Dozen apples

10 sacks of carrots

4 Bags of flour

1 Jar of strawberry jam

3 Bags chestnuts

5 onion

6 sacks

8 Loaves of

Phew! It's actually Mrs Claus' shopping list and NOT the precious GOOD list, but time is running out, Santa Claus will soon be setting off to deliver the Christmas presents.

If the reindeer were munching on the shopping list, perhaps Mrs Claus has taken the good list by mistake?

They can't find Mrs Claus in the Grotto though as she's left to go grocery shopping...

...and Santa is already clambering into the big red sleigh to check the GOOD list twice!

17

. . . . and Rusty jump into a snowmobile. Would they find Mrs Claus in time? If Santa doesn't leave exactly at the right time, he won't be able to deliver all the presents before Christmas Day!

At the store they skid to a halt in front of a very startled Mrs Claus and quickly explain the problem.

Mrs Claus puts on her glasses and looks at her list, "Oh no, this is a bit of a pickle but we can solve this problem together."

19

Mrs Claus calls Santa who booms "HO! HO! HO!" so loudly that it shakes the snow from the branches of the trees.

Santa zooms down in his sleigh to collect the priceless GOOD list and Rusty explains how GOOD

. . . .

has been to help unravel the Christmas chaos.

"Thank you very much . . . .,
it's always important to be good and helpful
and never naughty. You will definitely be
on my GOOD list this year," says a very
relieved and very thankful Santa Claus.

The end

COLOR ME IN →